Let's Count It Out, Jesse Bear

Let's Count It Out,
Jesse Bear

by Nancy White Carlstrom
illustrated by Bruce Degen

Simon & Schuster Books for Young Readers

OTHER JESSE BEAR BOOKS BY
NANCY WHITE CARLSTROM, ILLUSTRATED BY BRUCE DEGEN

Jesse Bear, What Will You Wear?
Better Not Get Wet, Jesse Bear
It's About Time, Jesse Bear
How Do You Say It Today, Jesse Bear?
Happy Birthday, Jesse Bear!

SIMON & SCHUSTER BOOKS FOR YOUNG READERS
An imprint of Simon & Schuster Children's Publishing Division
1230 Avenue of the Americas, New York, New York 10020
Text copyright © 1996 Nancy White Carlstrom
Illustrations copyright © 1996 Bruce DegenAll rights reserved including the right of
reproduction in whole or in part in any form.
SIMON & SCHUSTER BOOKS FOR YOUNG READERS is a trademark of Simon & Schuster.

Book design by Anahid Hamparian
The text for this book is set in 17-point Goudy Bold
The illustrations are rendered in pen and ink and watercolor

Printed and bound in the United States of America
First Edition
10 9 8 7 6 5 4 3 2 1

ISBN 0-689-80478-4
CIP data for this book is available from the Library of Congress

For the Bylsmas,
Linda, Pete, and Aaron
—N.W.C.

For Ben,
out to find out what really counts
—B.D.

One Is Fun

It started out a tickle
Deep down inside of me.
It turned into a giggle
And came out a Ha! Ha! Hee!
It romps and stomps
And roars about
Hurray! Hurrah! Hurroo!
And now—watch out!
It's coming—
One Silly will get you.

Ha! Ha! Hee!
Coming out of me.
Ha! Ha! Hoo!
Going after you.
It romps and stomps
And roars about
Hurray! Hurrah! Hurroo!
And now—watch out!
It's coming—
One Silly will get you.

None and one more is 1.
One is fun!

1 Silly

One Silly

2 Shoes

Two Shoes

Happy Hopping Two Shoes

Jesse Jesse two shoes
Jesse Jesse new shoes
Off he goes lickety-split
In lickety clickety shoes that fit.

Jumping high,
Landing loud.
New shoes dancing,
New shoes proud.

Rap-a-tap-a-tapping
Tip-a-tap-a-toeing
Stepping
Stopping
Sliding
Slowing
Happy hopping two shoes!

1
1 and one more are 2.
Happy hopping two shoes!

We Three

Who's in the picture place?
Squeezed in a tiny space,
Each with a funny face,
It's Mom and Dad and me!

What has our money bought?
Coming through the skinny slot,
A funny-faces snapshot—
It's Mom and Dad and me!

1, 2
2 and one more are 3.
We three!

3 Bears

Three Bears

Four that Roar

Thumping, bumping
Bumper car,
Goes real fast
But not too far.

Turn the wheel
And hold on tight.
Honk the horn
And blink the light.

Thumping, bumping
Slamming—*bam*!
Bumper cars
Are in a jam.

1, 2, 3
3 and one more are 4.
Four that roar!

4 **Bumper Cars**

Four **Bumper Cars**

Five Alive

Hello! Hello!
Anybody home?
Here comes one crab—
Are you all alone?
There by the water
Dances another.
Out of their holes
Poke sister and brother!

1, 2, 3, 4
4 and one more are 5.
Five alive!

5 Crabs

Five Crabs

Six Straight Sticks

A stick for throwing
And a stick for growing.

A stick for jumping
And a stick for dumping.

A stick for clicking
And a stick for licking.

1, 2, 3, 4, 5
5 and one more are 6.
Six straight sticks!

6 Sticks

Six Sticks

Seven in Heaven

Stars in the sky,
Stars in the tree.
How many stars
Shine down on me?

Six stars
Burning bright.
One more out,
It's a seven-star night.

1, 2, 3, 4, 5, 6
6 and one more are 7.
Seven in Heaven!

7 Stars

Seven Stars

Wait, There's Eight

The trouble with bubbles,
The trouble I see,
The bubbles go higher,
Much higher than me.
To the top of the roof,
To the top of the tree,
Those bubbles are flying
Sky-highing and free.
Now sailing on up
And out over the sea,
The trouble with bubbles,
They can't carry me.

1, 2, 3, 4, 5, 6, 7
7 and one more are 8.
Wait, there's eight!

8 Bubbles

Eight Bubbles

Nine Is Fine

Band-Aids are sticky
And such fun to wear
Band-Aids all over
Jesse Bear.

A scratch or a bump,
A lump or a cut,
Band-Aids are great
For fixing you up! Up! Up!

Band-Aids are great
For fixing you up!

1, 2, 3, 4, 5, 6, 7, 8
8 and one more are 9.
Nine is fine!

9 Band-Aids

Nine Band-Aids

Ten and Back Again

One is a smooth rock
Two is round
Three and Four
Today I found.
Five is purple
Six is rough
Seven and Eight
Would be enough.
But nine I'll give to Mommy soon,
And ten
Will be my little moon.

1, 2, 3, 4, 5, 6, 7, 8, 9
9 and one more are 10.
Ten and back again!

10 Rocks

Ten Rocks

10 and one more are **11.**
Eleven Clowns

11 and one more are **12.**
Twelve Hats

12 and one more are **13.**
Thirteen Flags

13 and one more are **14.**
Fourteen Wheels

14 and one more are **15.**
Fifteen Balls

15 and one more are **16.**
Sixteen Horns

16 and one more are **17.**
Seventeen Singers

17 and one more are **18.**
Eighteen Birds

18 and one more are **19.**
Nineteen Raindrops

19 and one more are **20.**
Twenty Ice-Cream Cones

PINEWOOD ELEMENTARY
1900 SE Pinewood Road